Copyright © 2020 Disney Enterprises, Inc.

All rights reserved. Published in the United States by Random House Children's Books,
a division of Penguin Random House LLC, 1745 Broadway, New York, NY 10019,
and in Canada by Penguin Random House Canada Limited, Toronto,
in conjunction with Disney Enterprises, Inc.

Random House and the colophon are registered trademarks of
Penguin Random House LLC.

rhcbooks.com

ISBN 978-0-7364-4084-4

Designed by Melanie Bermudez Cerna

MANUFACTURED IN CHINA
10 9 8 7 6 5 4 3 2 1

Disney
FROZEN

ALL AROUND ARENDELLE

By Elle Stephens

Illustrated by
the Disney Storybook Art Team

Random House 🏠 New York

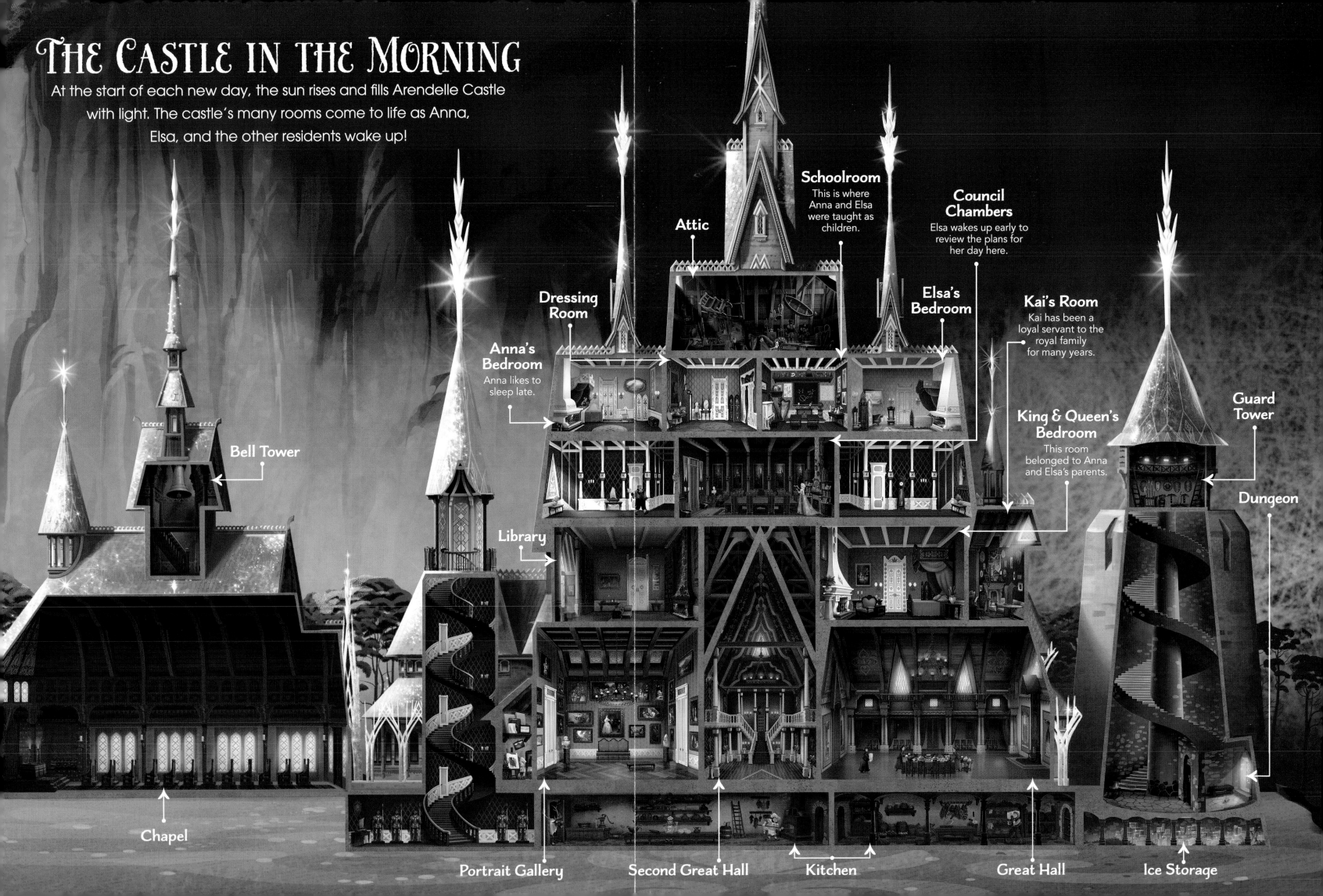

THE CASTLE IN THE MORNING

At the start of each new day, the sun rises and fills Arendelle Castle with light. The castle's many rooms come to life as Anna, Elsa, and the other residents wake up!

Schoolroom
This is where Anna and Elsa were taught as children.

Attic

Council Chambers
Elsa wakes up early to review the plans for her day here.

Dressing Room

Elsa's Bedroom

Anna's Bedroom
Anna likes to sleep late.

Kai's Room
Kai has been a loyal servant to the royal family for many years.

Bell Tower

King & Queen's Bedroom
This room belonged to Anna and Elsa's parents.

Guard Tower

Library

Dungeon

Chapel

Portrait Gallery

Second Great Hall

Kitchen

Great Hall

Ice Storage

Welcome to
ARENDELLE CASTLE!

This sparkling palace is home to Princess Anna and Queen Elsa. Their family has lived here for decades, but Elsa has recently added some icy touches to make it even more beautiful.

Let's go in and explore!

WHO LIVES IN THE CASTLE?

ELSA

As a child, Elsa had to hide her magical icy powers and feared leaving the castle. Now that she is Queen of Arendelle— and can control her powers and use them for the good of the kingdom—the castle finally feels like home.

ANNA

Anna has always loved exploring the castle and has had many adventures within its walls. She loves living here with Elsa and helping her sister rule the kingdom.

KRISTOFF

When Elsa left Arendelle, Kristoff helped Anna find her and bring her back home. Now he will always have a home in the castle—and a place in his heart for Anna.

OLAF

Elsa brought this happy snowman to life with her powers, and he loves living in the castle with his best friends, Anna, Elsa, Kristoff, and Sven. Elsa even gave him his own personal snow flurry to keep him from melting indoors!

SVEN

Sven is a reindeer and Kristoff's best friend. Kristoff rescued Sven when they were younger, and Sven helped Kristoff and Anna search for Elsa.

GERDA

Gerda has lived in the castle since before Anna and Elsa were born. She knows the castle better than anyone and has always taken good care of Anna and Elsa.

KAI

Kai has worked for the royal family for a very long time, overseeing the daily operations of the castle and keeping everything running smoothly.

OLINA

As head of the castle kitchen, Olina manages the kitchen staff and makes sure the royal family gets three healthy and delicious meals a day. Anna and Elsa have always loved her hot chocolate—especially after playing in the snow!

A colorful floral pattern
decorates the doors and furniture.

Anna likes to warm up beside
a cozy fire on chilly nights.

Anna has a painting
of Arendelle Castle on her wall.

Anna has a dressing area
to prepare for royal events.

Sometimes Anna
has a special visitor—
a sleepy cat!

Anna loves to read.
She keeps a trunk full of
books and cozy blankets.

Anna's Bedroom

Anna loves company, but
she also needs a cozy space
of her own. Her bedroom is
decorated in warm pink
and rose tones, with plush
bedding and rugs.
She loves to relax here!

As children, Anna and Elsa
used to share a bedroom.
But that changed when
Elsa accidentally hurt
Anna with her magic.

❧ A Special Surprise ❧

Anna and Elsa eat breakfast together every morning. One day, Elsa told Anna she had a surprise for her.

"I love surprises!" said Anna. "What is it?"

"Well, if I told you, it wouldn't be a surprise," replied Elsa. "But it's waiting for you in your room right now."

Anna jumped up from the table, knocking over her water glass. Luckily, Elsa was able to freeze the water in midair before it spilled all over the table.

Within seconds, Anna was running down the hall to her bedroom. She threw the door open and began to search for her surprise. She looked behind her pillows and under the covers. She checked above the canopy and under the bed, then around her dressing screen. But she still didn't see a surprise.

Anna was about to crawl into the fireplace, when Elsa came in and saw the mess Anna had made in her room.

"What are you doing?" Elsa asked her sister.

"I'm looking for my hidden surprise," said Anna.

"I didn't hide your surprise, silly," replied Elsa. "It's right there."

She pointed to the wall near Anna's dressing screen, where a beautiful painting of Arendelle now hung.

Anna gasped. She loved it! "It's so beautiful!" she exclaimed, hugging her sister. "Thank you so much!"

"My pleasure," said Elsa. "Now let's get this room cleaned up!"

THE DRESSING ROOM

Anna and Elsa share a dressing room, where they keep all the gowns they need for their royal events and duties. This is also where they keep accessories, like cloaks, hats, sashes, and tiaras.

Anna and Elsa use this dressing screen when they change outfits.

The room is always brightly lit.

There is plenty of storage space for hats and accessory boxes.

Kai makes sure Anna's and Elsa's newest items are carefully delivered to the dressing room and put away.

Royal seamstresses use a dress form to hold gowns in place while they sew new outfits together.

A golden chandelier casts warm light over the hall.

The balconies provide an excellent view of the festivities below.

Music always sounds wonderful in this large, open space!

There is plenty of room for guests to mingle and dance.

Thanks to Elsa's icy powers, the Great Hall has featured indoor snowstorms and even an ice-skating rink!

Elsa stands by her throne to greet her guests.

Tables of delicious food and drinks are set up in the Great Hall whenever there's a celebration.

THE GREAT HALL

With its high ceilings and

hand-painted murals,

the Great Hall provides

a beautiful setting

for everything from

official meetings to

grand balls and parties.

❖ A Great Time ❖

One evening, Elsa was hosting a big celebration in the Great Hall.

It was filled with guests dining, dancing, and having a wonderful time.

In the corner, a band played a lively song.

But Elsa noticed that someone was missing.

"Olaf," she said, "have you seen Anna? She was so excited to dance tonight, but I haven't seen her anywhere."

"I'll find her!" Olaf volunteered. He walked out onto the dance floor and looked between all the couples, who were whirling and swirling to the music. No Anna.

He checked around the buffet table and even underneath it. Still no Anna.

He found a group of people sitting near the band and was sure that Anna would be with them. But she wasn't there, either.

Olaf was beginning to worry. Then he remembered something.

"The balcony!" he exclaimed. "Anna loves it up there." He ran to the balcony, where he found Anna flying back and forth on a swing that hung in one of the windows.

A few moments later, Olaf returned to Elsa.

"Did you find Anna?" Elsa asked the snowman.

"I sure did!" He pointed to the balcony. "She has the best seat in the house!" ❧

THE SECOND GREAT HALL

The Second Great Hall is where royal guests go when they arrive at the castle. With its high wooden ceiling, regal banners, and grand staircase, it's the perfect place for Elsa to greet her visitors.

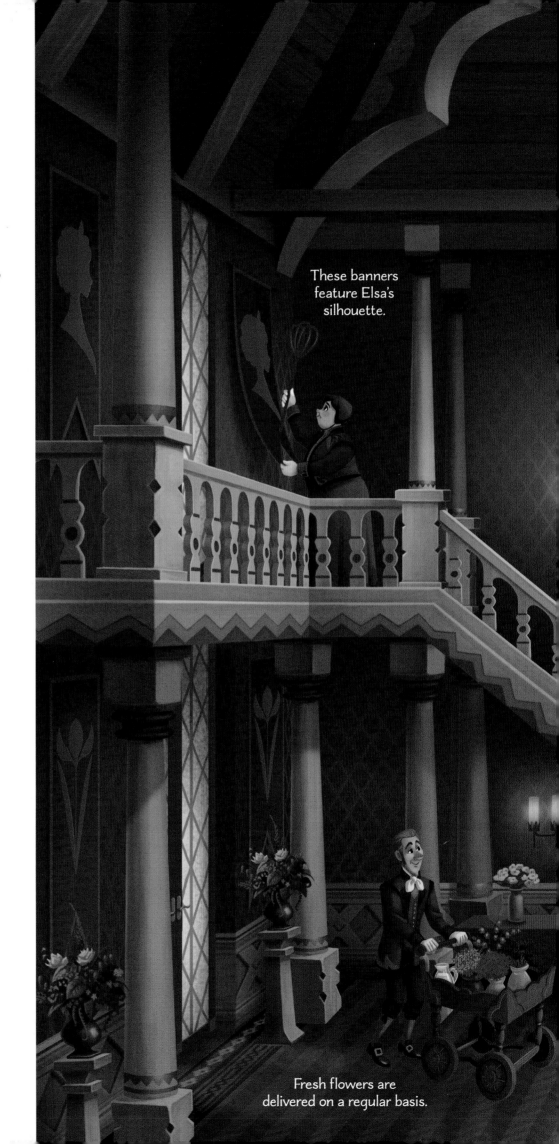

These banners feature Elsa's silhouette.

Fresh flowers are delivered on a regular basis.

This banner features a crocus, the official flower of Arendelle.

These are the stairs that Anna and Elsa once rode their tandem bike down!

Elsa makes a grand entrance when she comes down these stairs!

These doors lead out to the castle courtyard. This is where important guests and visitors are greeted.

Anna used to love pretending she was the one being pushed on the swing in this painting.

This room includes royal sculptures as well.

This royal family portrait was painted when Anna and Elsa were very young.

No one is sure who this relative is, but Anna really likes his beard.

Sven likes this room, too!

THE PORTRAIT GALLERY

Paintings of all the royal family members and people important to the history of Arendelle hang in the Portrait Gallery. This has always been one of Anna's favorite rooms.

⤷ FRIENDLY PORTRAITS ⤶

One afternoon, Anna invited Kristoff to the Portrait Gallery.

"Growing up, I thought of all the people in these paintings as my friends," Anna explained. "So I wanted you to meet them."

She led Kristoff from painting to painting. "This guy loves his hat." Anna pointed to a portrait of a man in a tall hat. "And this couple is madly in love." She climbed onto the sofa to get closer to a painting of a man kissing a woman's hand.

"Nice to meet you," said Kristoff.

Anna pointed to a painting of two little girls. "That's me and Elsa when we were younger." Then she pointed to a sculpture of a man with a long beard. "And that's our great-uncle Henrik."

Just then, Anna and Kristoff heard a "Hmmph!"

"Umm," said Kristoff, looking around, "does Great-Uncle Henrik usually talk to you?"

Perplexed, Anna leaned closer to the sculpture.

"Hmmph!" they heard again. This time the noise had come from behind the door.

"Who's out there?" called Kristoff.

The door slowly opened to reveal Sven pushing his way into the Portrait Gallery.

"Hi, buddy!" said Kristoff. "Do you want to meet Anna's friends, too?"

Anna gave the reindeer a big hug. "These paintings are great, but I'd much rather spend time with the two of you!"

THE LIBRARY

Anna and Elsa both love
to read, so the library is one
of their favorite rooms.
In addition to keeping many
wonderful stories on its
shelves, the library also
holds the history of Arendelle.
Anna and Elsa come here
whenever they need help
solving a royal problem or
want to better understand
their kingdom.

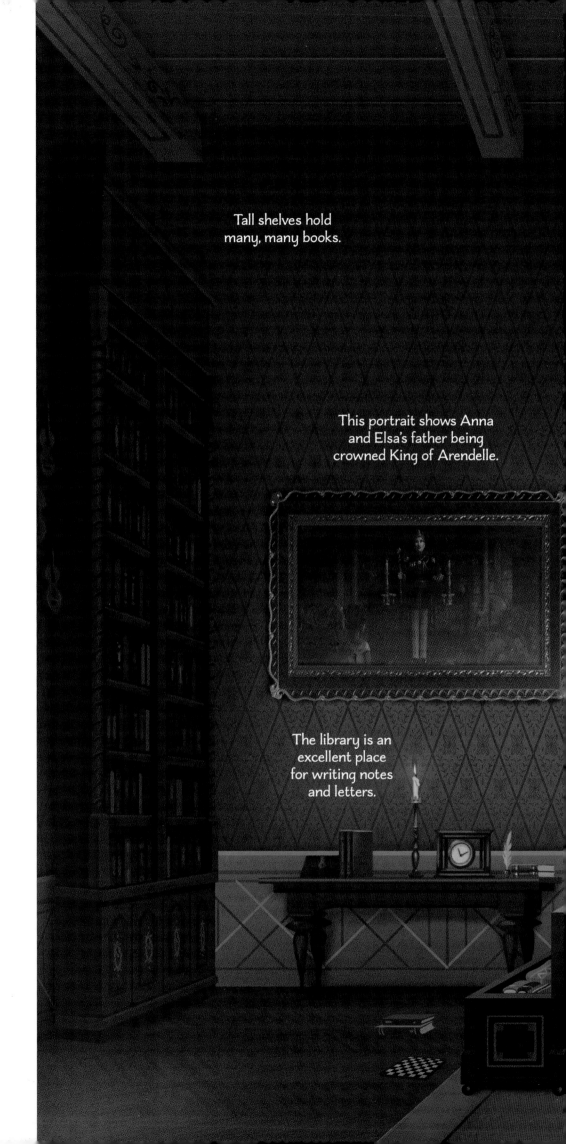

Tall shelves hold
many, many books.

This portrait shows Anna
and Elsa's father being
crowned King of Arendelle.

The library is an
excellent place
for writing notes
and letters.

Olaf loves the library—
especially the fireplace!

This comfy chaise is the
perfect spot to curl up
with a book.

A fireplace keeps
the room warm
and cozy.

❖ Book Club ❖

One afternoon, Olaf found Kristoff outside the castle library, jiggling the handles of its heavy wooden doors.

"Ooh!" exclaimed Olaf. "Are you playing a game?"

"I wish," said Kristoff. "I accidentally locked a book in the library."

"But don't books *belong* in the library?" asked Olaf.

"Well, yes, but not this one. See, Anna has been reading this book she really loves. So while she and Elsa were out, I snuck into her room to borrow it and brought it down to read in the library. But when I got up to get a snack, the doors locked behind me. Now I have to get Anna's book before she's back."

"Oh, I can help you!" Olaf said excitedly. He took off his carrot nose and shoved the pointed end into the lock on the door. He wiggled it

around until he heard a *click.* "Ta-da!" he exclaimed as the doors opened.

"Olaf, you're a hero! A book hero!" cheered Kristoff.

Just then, Anna appeared in the doorway. "Oh, I'm so happy to see you both so excited about my favorite book!" she exclaimed.

"We can't wait to read it!" Kristoff and Olaf said together.

THE ATTIC

The castle attic is where
Anna and Elsa's family
treasures are stored.
The space is warm
and dry, so it keeps
special items safe.

Paintings that don't
fit in the Portrait
Gallery can be
stored here.

The attic is home to
old books that don't
fit in the library.

Anna and Elsa loved to ride this bicycle.

Some of the instruments that Anna and Elsa learned to play during music lessons are here.

Olaf has fun trying on suits of armor stored here.

Anna and Elsa's sled was once the fastest in the kingdom!

Anna and Elsa each have a special trunk filled with items from their childhood.

❧ ATTIC TREASURES ❧

One day, Anna and Elsa were looking for Olaf. They had searched everywhere but the attic, so they decided to look there.

"Olaf?" they called into the dusty room. They heard a *creak* from a corner and turned to see an old suit of armor.

"Did that just move?" asked Anna. Just then, the armor's helmet fell off and Olaf poked his head out from the suit.

"Anna! Elsa! I'm stuck!" he cried.

"We'll get you out," said Anna.

"But what are you doing up here?" asked Elsa.

"Well, I lost my lucky rock, so I came here to look for it. But then I saw this suit of armor and wanted to try it on," explained Olaf.

"We'll help you look for your rock," said Anna.

Together, the three found some old toys.

"Do you remember this rocking horse?" asked Elsa.

"Of course!" said Anna. "And do you remember this sled?"

An hour later, all they had found was lots of fun memories.

"What does your rock look like, again?" asked Anna.

"Like this!" said Olaf, holding up the rock they had been searching for.

"When did you find it?" asked Elsa.

"About an hour ago," replied Olaf. "But we were having so much fun going through your old stuff, I didn't want to stop!"

Royal tapestries
decorate the
room and help to
keep it warm.

The table is long enough
to seat the entire council,
and Elsa always sits
at the head.

This globe provides
a map of the world
and a place to store
royal letters.

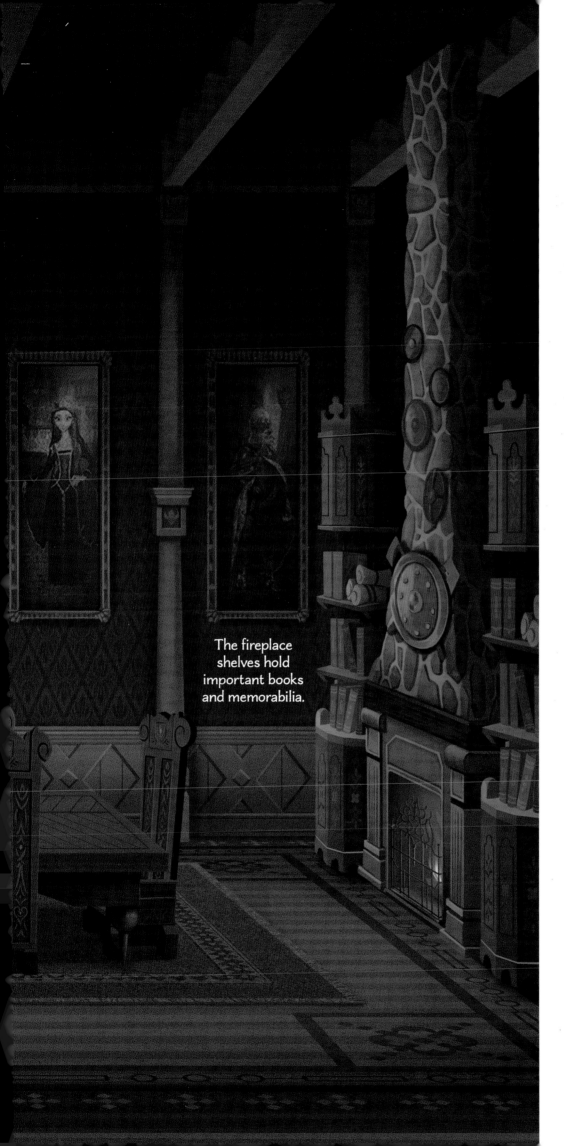

The fireplace shelves hold important books and memorabilia.

THE COUNCIL CHAMBERS

Queen Elsa holds important royal discussions and meetings in the Council Chambers. She and the Arendelle Council meet with foreign ambassadors and make official decisions here, and this is also where her parents held family meetings when she and Anna were younger.

❖ Secret Chambers ❖

One afternoon, Anna wanted to play hide-and-seek with Elsa, but Elsa was busy with royal paperwork in the Council Chambers.

"I'll hide," said Anna. "You can come and find me when you're done."

Elsa signed several scrolls, then opened the globe and placed them in the hidden compartment inside. She looked up at the paintings of her ancestors on the walls.

"Did you have to do this much paperwork?" she asked them.

"Nope," came a reply. "And neither should you!"

Elsa recognized the voice right away. "Anna? Where are you?"

"You have to find me!" replied Anna. "It's hide-and-seek, remember?"

Elsa looked under the table, then behind the globe.

"You're getting closer," said Anna.

"You can see me?" asked Elsa. Just then, she saw something move behind one of the paintings.

Anna was in a secret passage behind the painting, watching her through the eyes in the picture!

"Found you!" Elsa shouted, victorious.

"Only if you can figure out how I got back here!" Anna responded.

"You're on!" Elsa said.

THE KITCHEN

The castle kitchen is stocked with food from the kingdom's farms and gardens. The kitchen staff works hard to keep the royal family, castle staff, and visitors well-fed.

Sven often comes to the kitchen looking for carrots.

Buckets of fresh water are used for cooking and cleaning produce.

Fresh fruits and vegetables are delivered daily.

The kitchen is stocked with a variety of pots and pans.

Fresh breads and pastries are baked daily.

The castle baker rolls out dough for his latest creation.

The bell keeper takes care of the bell and rings it when needed.

The chapel is decorated with rosemaling, a traditional art form in Arendelle.

A priest lights the chapel candles and leads the coronation ceremony.

Rows of wooden benches can hold many guests.

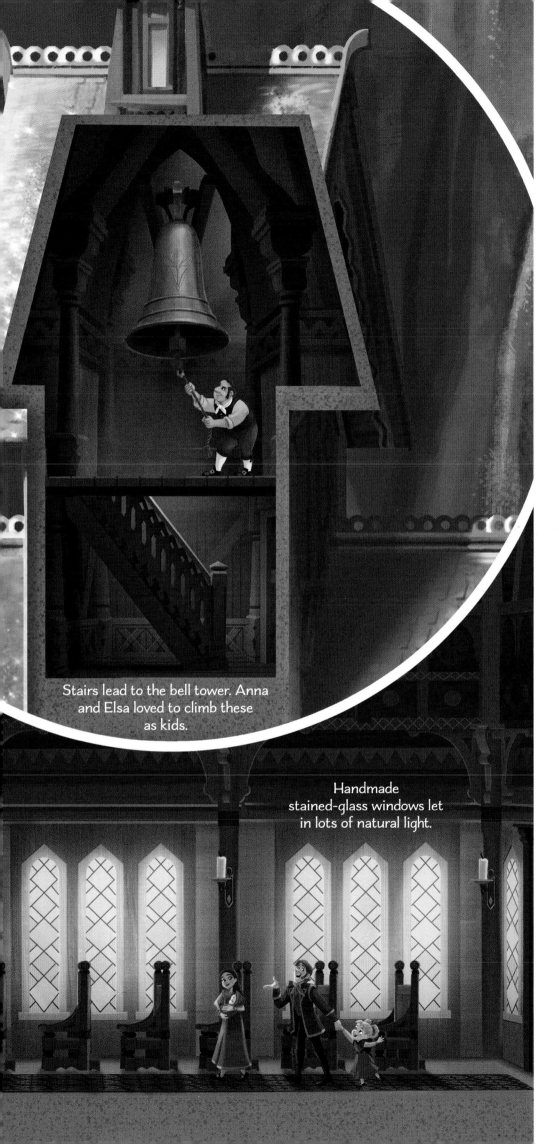

Stairs lead to the bell tower. Anna
and Elsa loved to climb these
as kids.

Handmade
stained-glass windows let
in lots of natural light.

THE CHAPEL

The royal chapel is located
next to the castle. This is where
coronation ceremonies are
held whenever a new ruler
is crowned. The most
recent one was Elsa's!

THE BELL TOWER

The bell tower atop the
chapel is one of the highest
structures in Arendelle.
The large bell there is rung
for special occasions.

ELSA'S BEDROOM

After a busy day fulfilling her royal duties, Elsa needs a private space where she can relax. Decorated in cool blues and purples, her bedroom is a calm and welcoming place to unwind.

A painting of Arendelle Castle hangs on Elsa's wall, just like in Anna's room.

Elsa creates ice sculptures as decorations.

In addition to their shared dressing room, Elsa has a dressing area of her own, where she keeps gowns and prepares for special events.

Elsa's bedroom is decorated with rosemaling.

Elsa's canopy bed is warm and cozy.

Elsa loves to read and write here on this soft rug.

❖ Bedtime for Elsa ❖

Every evening, Elsa spends time relaxing in her bedroom before she goes to sleep. One night, she heard a knock on her door and opened it to find Olaf.

"Come on in," said Elsa, happy to see her friend. "What are you doing still up?"

"I couldn't sleep," said Olaf, "so I wanted to know what you usually do when you're trying to get sleepy."

Elsa giggled. "Well, first I put on my pajamas. Then I sit by the fire and read for a bit."

"That sounds cozy," said Olaf.

"When I start to feel drowsy, I get in my bed and look at this painting." Elsa pointed to a painting on her bedroom wall. It showed the ice palace she had made high on the North Mountain.

"Mmm, that's beautiful," said Olaf.

"Yes, it's my favorite," said Elsa. As she turned to Olaf, she heard snoring. He had fallen fast asleep.

"I guess my bedtime routine works!" she said. ❖

THE CASTLE AT NIGHT

Each night, the castle staff cleans up and prepares for bedtime.
They make sure the fires are lit in Anna's and Elsa's rooms so
the sisters have a warm, cozy place to sleep.

Anna's Bedroom
Olina turns down the covers on Anna's bed.

Elsa's Bedroom
Gerda makes sure Elsa has enough pillows on her bed.

Council Chambers
The Council Chamber is quiet after a busy day.

Great Hall
The castle staff cleans up the Great Hall and blows out the candles after a royal dinner.

Library
Anna, Elsa, Kristoff, and Sven often spend evenings together here.

Kitchen

All around ARENDELLE CASTLE!

Anna and Elsa opened the castle gates once Elsa became queen, and they haven't closed them since! Outside the castle, the kingdom of Arendelle bustles as the people go about their day.

Let's go out and explore!

Arendelle is located on the edge of a fjord—an inlet surrounded by high cliffs.

With a queen who can control ice, any time of year is the perfect time for ice-skating and playing in the snow!

The crocus is the official flower of Arendelle. It adorns much of the kingdom. The flower can bloom in snow.

When frozen, this harbor is perfect for ice-skating.

Each street has lots of colorful houses and buildings.

Fish is part of the Arendelle diet, along with fruits and vegetables.

The citizens use logs to keep warm during the winter.

Olaf's First Day of School

One of Olaf's favorite things to do was explore Arendelle. He wanted to know everything there was to know about his new home. He wanted to see everything, from the clock tower to the harbor, and he loved learning new things.

While strolling around the town, Olaf saw a group of children walking in a line.

"A parade!" Olaf squealed. "I love parades! But why are you taking your parade inside when it's so nice outside?" he asked one of them.

"It's not a parade," a girl named Lisbet replied, giggling. "We're on our way to school." She headed inside, where most of the other children already were.

Olaf had never been to a school. He gazed through the window, where he saw the children seating themselves at neat rows of wooden desks.

A kind-looking woman smiled and greeted

each child from the front of the room. Then she saw Olaf. "Hello there!" she said to him. "I'm Ms. Halvorson." She told him she was the teacher. "Our class is about to begin. Would you like to join us?"

"Really?" Olaf asked. "Could I?"

"Of course! We'd love to have you," Ms. Halvorson replied.

Olaf asked what he had to do as part of her class.

The teacher asked him, "What do you like to do?"

Olaf thought about his answer. "I like to learn new things," he said.

Ms. Halvorson smiled and showed him to an open desk beside Lisbet. "If you enjoy learning, then you've definitely come to the right place!"

THE ROYAL GARDENS

Anna and Elsa love to spend time outdoors in the royal gardens. There are games to play, flowers to smell, and a beautiful field to relax on in the warmer months. Olaf loves being able to come here with everyone!

Sometimes people blow fuzz off dandelions to make a wish. What do you think Elsa is wishing for?

What would *you* wish for?

Anna couldn't resist joining in on chasing butterflies!

In the summer, Arendelle's days are extra long, which means more time to play outside!

Look how proud this Mother Duck is of her four ducklings—make that five, with the last one in the line!

Elsa's magic keeps Olaf from melting so he can go out and about during summer!

Wandering Oaken's Trading Post and Sauna has all your seasonal needs, for any weather. Vegetables, snowshoes, umbrellas—and a sun balm of Oaken's own invention!

Oaken's shelves feature everything from apples and carrots and cheese to a boat! Although, the boat is technically not on a shelf. . . .

Oaken loves inventing new things, like the sun balm and cough remedies he sells here.

Here are the towels for the sauna, where it gets really hot!

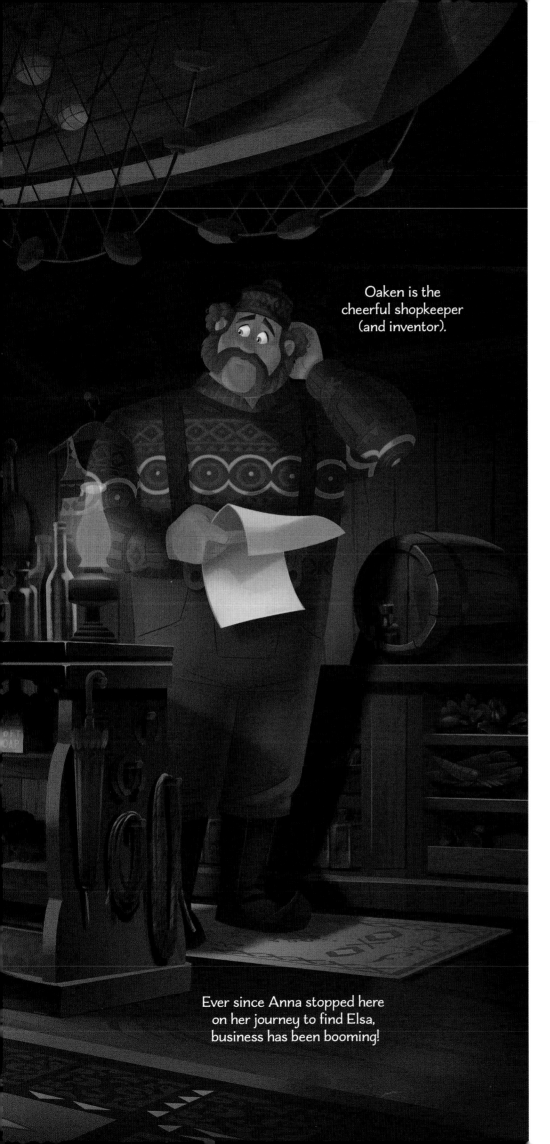

Oaken is the cheerful shopkeeper (and inventor).

Ever since Anna stopped here on her journey to find Elsa, business has been booming!

OAKEN'S TRADING POST AND SAUNA

"Hoo, hoo!" A short hike to the mountains above Arendelle and the castle, one can find Wandering Oaken's Trading Post and Sauna. Oaken's store is stocked with all sorts of merchandise for surviving the Arendelle winters, including his own inventions!

✣ THE OAKEN ✣ FAMILY REUNION

Oaken loved inventing new things, almost as much as he loved his family. And it was time for Oaken's entire family to visit him!

Everyone's favorite family tradition was the Creators Contest, during which Oaken and his family shared their inventions since their last reunion. Oaken had previously invented a cough remedy that had helped his cousins feel better, but this year, he couldn't think of anything new to invent. In need of a break, Oaken headed outside to his sauna—and slipped on some ice blocks.

"*Uff da!*" Oaken yelped as the ice began to slide down the mountain. Oaken followed the ice and noticed that the block started to glow. He looked up and saw the Northern Lights. When he looked at the block again, he realized that the colors in the sky made the ice appear to glow from within.

Oaken hurried back to his shop. He knew what to invent for the Creators Contest!

Oaken's family arrived the next day and greeted each other with a "Hoo, hoo!" After playing and eating, they shared their inventions in the Creators Contest. Grandma Hedda's sweater with earmuffs attached by a string would keep everything warm at once. Uncle Soren's unusually bent piece of metal would hold papers together.

For Oaken's invention, everyone had to follow him outside into the dark night. They could see a massive block of ice in the center of a clearing. When the Northern Lights emerged in the sky, bright bursts of color erupted everywhere from the ice. It was the most beautiful thing they had ever seen—and it was perfect for celebrating a family reunion!

VALLEY OF THE LIVING ROCK

When Anna was struck with a frozen heart on her search to help Elsa, she and Kristoff visited the trolls in the Valley of the Living Rock. The trolls had raised Kristoff and Sven when they were little. During the day, they looked like mossy boulders, but at night, they woke up!

The trolls hold an annual crystal ceremony each autumn under the Northern Lights.

Kristoff was raised by the trolls in this valley. This is his childhood home!

Brock told Anna her parents asked Grand Pabbie to remove her memories of Elsa's magic.

Bulda is Kristoff's adoptive mother.

Anna, Elsa, Kristoff, Sven, and Olaf helped Little Rock earn his tracking crystal.

Grand Pabbie is the wise old leader of the trolls. He once told Anna that only an act of true love could thaw her frozen heart.

❧ TROLLSITTING ❧

Anna and Kristoff were on their way to the Valley of the Living Rock, where they were going to babysit the littlest trolls. Kristoff reminisced about growing up there with the trolls, and told Anna how Bulda, his adoptive mother, had a strict bedtime for all the young trolls. "So they'll probably be asleep the whole time," he said. "We'll spend the evening relaxing by the fire."

When they arrived, Bulda said to Kristoff, "It seems like just yesterday that *you* were young enough to have a sitter!"

After the older trolls left, the baby trolls were up for anything *except* sleep. They climbed and ran all over!

"No, no, no!" Anna said, hurrying to grab a couple of troll tots that were climbing some boulders. "That's dangerous!"

Kristoff encountered a leaning tower of trolls that had climbed on each other's backs. "Let's settle down, now," he said as he took each troll down.

Anna and Kristoff tried to feed the
troll babies smashed berries, and
checked their leaf diapers, but it
seemed like the more they tried to
do, the wilder the trolls got. Then
they heard a new voice.

"Hello, troll babies!" It was Olaf!

Anna went to greet the snowman,
and in her hurry, tripped and fell face-first
into the basket of smashed berries. When
she lifted her head, her face was dripping
with purple goop!

The little trolls raced over and
lapped the berry juice from her
face. "Well, I guess that's one way
to feed them!" Kristoff said.

THE ICE PALACE

When Elsa froze the kingdom of Arendelle into an eternal winter, she created the ice palace to escape from those who feared her powers. While love thawed a frozen heart and Elsa was able to unfreeze Arendelle, the ice palace still stands high in the mountains above the town, and is home to the snowgies and Marshmallow.

Elsa made the palace entirely out of ice. After all, the cold never bothered her anyway!

Marshmallow protected Elsa
when she didn't want vistors.
He still lives at the palace
with the snowgies.

Elsa built this stairway
before she built the
rest of the palace.

❖ THE ICE PALACE ❖

Not far from Arendelle Castle, high up on the North Mountain, is the ice palace. A giant snowman named Marshmallow lived here, along with a bunch of teeny, tiny snowmen called snowgies.

One day, Olaf went to visit them.

"Hi, Marshmallow!" he called. "Isn't it exciting that we have all these little brothers now?"

Marshmallow sighed. He looked very tired. He got up and went outside, leaving Olaf with the snowgies, who were piled in a mound in a corner.

"Hi, little guys!" said Olaf. He tried to hug them, but the snowgies jumped off their pile and ran out, too. Olaf chased some of them, but they were too fast.

When Olaf got outside, he saw that Marshmallow was building a playpen out of icicles around the snowgies. But they snuck out before he could finish! They formed a line at the top of the palace stairs to slide down the banister.

"Uh, be careful, guys!" called Olaf. But the snowgies weren't listening. They flew down the banister in groups of two and three. An hour went by, then another hour, and they were still sliding. Olaf grew tired just watching them.

Finally, Marshmallow opened the palace doors. Exhausted, the snowgies ran inside and jumped back into a pile in the corner. Soon they were all fast asleep.

"You guys sure know how to have fun!" Olaf said as he left. He made sure the palace doors were shut tightly before he headed back to Arendelle Castle for a good night's sleep. ❧

King Agnarr, Anna and Elsa's father, used to tell stories of the Arendellians and the Northuldra, who were trapped in the forest.

The Enchanted Forest is surrounded by a mist that allows no one in or out. However, Anna and Elsa and their friends were able to enter.

Olaf told his friends that water has memory. That explains how Elsa's ice powers could help reveal the past.

THE ENCHANTED FOREST

When Elsa is called to the Enchanted Forest to find answers, Anna, Kristoff, Sven, and Olaf go with her. They encounter new people, new stories, and new magic.

Thank you for visiting

ARENDELLE!

Anna and Elsa are always happy
to share their royal home with friends.